William F. Warren

The story of Gottlieb

William F. Warren

The story of Gottlieb

ISBN/EAN: 9783743333703

Manufactured in Europe, USA, Canada, Australia, Japa

Cover: Foto ©Andreas Hilbeck / pixelio.de

Manufactured and distributed by brebook publishing software
(www.brebook.com)

William F. Warren

The story of Gottlieb

THE "KOENIGSSTUHL" AT HEIDELBERG.

The
Story of Gottlieb

BY

WILLIAM F. WARREN

PRESIDENT OF BOSTON UNIVERSITY

MEADVILLE PENN'A
FLOOD AND VINCENT
The Chautauqua-Century Press
M DCCC XCII

The Chautauqua-Century Press, Meadville, Pa., U. S. A.
Electrotyped, Printed, and Bound by Flood and Vincent.

TO

STUDENTS AND TEACHERS

OF

IDEALS IN PERSONAL LIVING

This Little Parable

IS

RESPECTFULLY DEDICATED

Prefatory Note.

This story, first told to some of my students in Boston, has since been retold in the Arabic tongue to the mountaineers in Lebanon.

A German professor, who received his doctorate in the University at Heidelberg, has asked permission to publish a German translation, and is now engaged in its preparation.

W. F. W.

THE STORY OF GOTTLIEB

THE STORY OF GOTTLIEB.

GOTTLIEB was a German youth, well born and well brought up in Bingen on the Rhine. Full of life, he loved the hills and woods, the playgrounds and the river. In all the sports he easily excelled. Lessons he could easily learn, and to equal a classmate or to win the approbation of a favorite teacher, he would often show his readiness as a scholar. Still in serious studies of any kind he had little interest until his seventeenth year. That summer an elder sister, whose home was in Vienna, returned after years of absence to Bingen to visit her parents and the tall Gottlieb, whom she had left a growing boy.

She was a woman of high literary attainment and of still higher moral enthusiasm.

It happened that at this very time she was engaged in a literary pilgrimage. Her plan was to visit in succession every town and city of Germany in which the poet Goethe had ever lived, and there upon the spot to read whatever in his works or in his biographies would serve to illustrate the experiences of the poet at the time of his sojourn or the effects of those experiences upon his subsequent character, history, and writings.

With Gottlieb she was delighted beyond measure. To her affectionate eye he seemed so noble in feature and form, so fresh and beautiful in spirit, that she was continually saying to herself, "It must be! it must be! He, too, is a son of genius, and heir to the world's honors. At seventeen Goethe himself cannot have been a more perfect type of noble human powers and possibilities." The more she drew him out to determine, if she could, the special bent of his mind and the quality of his tastes, the more was she fascinated with the variety of his gifts, the keenness of his insight, and the simple naturalness of his whole mental life. Happy days they spent together at home and in long rambles on the mountains and in the valleys outside the town. Each was an inspiration to the other. The boy had never before come in contact with a mind so keenly alive to everything beautiful and ennobling. His honest deference to her wider knowledge, his childlike admiration of her larger life, gave to the sister a freedom and earnestness and enthusiasm of utterance which were at times a surprise to herself.

But with this complacent surprise she could not stop. The conviction that this young spirit was destined to as proud a pre-eminence among men as the immortal poet whom she so passionately admired, left her no inclination to think of herself. The hours were precious. She determined that she would open to him the gates of the new life at whose threshold he was standing. She would kindle his yet unkindled ambition, arouse his unsuspecting powers to self-discovery, fill him with quenchless aspira-

tions for the good, the beautiful, the true. So
on and on she talked and charmed him into
talking; voicing literature, nature, human life;
teaching him by unstudied example how wondrously the poet's eye and word can give
interpretation to the sunset, to the march of
marshaled stars and swell of the growing moon;
how yet more wondrously, by deeper and more
secret sympathies, noble souls can enter and
explore the life of other souls, yea, of all souls,
and in creations deathless as Homer's song or
the "Divina Commedia" of Dante, voice for
endless ages even the unconscious thought and
life of man. At times she longed to turn upon
him more directly, and with sisterly authority
and affection summon him to dedicate his life
to the lofty purpose of seeking knowledge, ideal
experiences, personal perfection. A truer instinct, however, always assured her that if he
was indeed the rare spirit she had taken him to
be, a thorough wakening of his faculties would
suffice, and that a self-taken resolution to rise to
the loftiest altitudes of life would be more effect-

ive than any bare assent to high suggestions from without.

At the end of the visit she was gratified to find she had not misjudged. Their last afternoon they climbed together the Scharlachkopf and lingered near the conspicuous church of St. Roch until the sun descended behind a strange series of cloudy bars, by which the whole broad valley and river were streaked with alternations of fading light and shadow.

Returning homeward in the gloaming, she was filled with pride and pleasure as Gottlieb suddenly stopped in the way, and exclaimed, "Sister Gretchen, your coming has made an epoch in my life. This Rhine river, these Bingen hills and stars, can never again be to me what they were. Life now has meaning. I am an immortal spirit, set in the living center of a boundless universe. The trees may sleep and the birds dream, but such a life is not for so god-like a nature as man's. For him, one thing alone is fitting—that one thing is the intelligent, the ardent, the endless pursuit of perfection.

The instinct is in me, and to it I **will be true. I
will live for** nothing lower **or** less. **It is the**
voice of nature, it is the mandate of God. And,
believe me, in all my efforts to redeem this vow,
I will ever be mindful of the debt I owe to you.
I will ever cherish your **image with grateful**
affection and draw from **your sisterly love a
sacred inspiration."**

Three years later Gottlieb **was nearing the
close** of **his university** studies at Heidelberg.
Those years had fully attested the **genuineness**
and thoroughness **of the change which had
come over the young** man's life. **His** enthusi-
asm for all things loftiest **in** character and
attainment had been in him a motive to appli-
cation almost measureless in power and practi-
cally unremitting. In acquisition of knowledge
and growth of faculty **he had** manifestly dis-
tanced all **who had** started with him. Withal
he had done it in such a large-hearted and
apparently **unconscious manner that** no one
seemed to cherish toward him any feeling save

that of heartiest admiration. His wealth of thought, range of interest, clearness of ideas, and force of character made him everywhere a man of mark among his fellows, and drew to him in friendly fellowship some of the choicest spirits among his instructors. He had drawn great inspiration from the life and words of his sister's poet ; greater yet from those immortal philosophers and teachers who had refused to subordinate the ethical to the æsthetic. He yearned for all beauty and all truth, and claimed that without inherence in the good neither the beautiful nor the true was possible.

One Saturday his solitary walk had taken him to the top of the tower on Koenigsstuhl, the mountain to the rear of the town, whence there was a favorite view of the broad Rhine valley as it slopes far northward and then westward toward distant Bingen. A long time his eye lingered upon the waning sunset, noting the transformations of cloud and shadow, and especially struck by certain peculiar bands of light that reminded him of the similar ones

noticed on that memorable night of his parting
with Sister Gretchen. A wonderful quiet, too,
was in the tree tops that swept away adown the
wooded slopes below him. It reminded him of
the indescribable pathos with which, on that
same bright day, Gretchen had recited Goethe's
lines, written upon the Wartburg,—

" *Ueber allen Gipfeln ist Ruh.*"

Happy in all the meditations and memories
of the sacred hour, he returned to his room to
write to her his customary letter of affectionate
remembrance. As he entered, a telegram from
Vienna was lying upon the table. It brought
news of the sudden death of her who had been
such a high priestess of life to his boyish soul,
such a treasure to his manly heart. Stunned
by the unexpected blow, he sank into a chair
and wished himself also dead. The next moment, true to his critical habit, he found himself
asking whether it were right and fitting for a
seeker of personal perfection ever to wish himself dead. Then desperately angry at himself
for such an attempted analysis of a sacred and

heartrending grief, he hid his face in his hands and sobbed like a child.

Next day, late in the evening, he was in Vienna. As in a dream he played his part in the spectral panorama of the funeral obsequies. As in a dream he saw kindred and strangers meet and part. As in a dream he found the purpose of his journey accomplished and nothing remaining for him to do but to return to the place of his studies. This, however, he felt he could not as yet do. The world had suddenly changed. He felt himself moving in a mysterious maze. His old conception of life had had in it no place for death and desolation. He had studied only the perfect, the ideal, and the means of its attainment. He had coveted something for which the universe now seemed to have no tolerance—a perfect life. To give himself time to recover from his stupefaction, he resolved to make his return journey a leisurely one, through the valley of the upper Danube, with such stops and sojourns as might best suit his moods and crippled resolutions. So doing, as in

a kind of somnambulism, he paid his fare to
Salzburg and arriving at that quaint old city,
took lodgings in the inn "Zum Goldenen
Schiff."

Perhaps the quaintest and most romantic
churchyard in Central Europe is that of St.
Peter's at Salzburg. Itself gardenlike, it is
nestled under a towering cliff, in whose perpen-
dicular face full half a hundred feet above the
observer is a cave now fitted up as a chapel in
memory of a prehistoric saint, Maximus by
name, who more than a thousand years ago,
when Germany was yet largely heathen ground
here lodged and prayed and fasted. To reach it
steps and passages are cut in the solid rock, with
here and there outlooks for the ascending pil-
grim. Below, built against the base of the rock-
mountain are long arcades of masonry, with
tombs for families of wealth and distinction. In
one of these sleeps all that was mortal of the
great composer Haydn, and in adjacent ground
is buried Baroness Sonnenberg, a sister of Mo-
zart. For hundreds of years the spot has been a

place of holy meditation to the living, a home of perfect peace to the dead.

We cannot wonder that this beautiful and sacred ground exercised upon Gottlieb a singular charm. Nor is it strange that the new-made grave he there discovered so much reminded him of the one he had left in Vienna that at different times he returned to it to meditate and to wrestle with the mystery which had invaded his soul. The third day, in the afternoon, the mother of the girl who filled this new-made grave came to bring fresh flowers, and to lighten her own heavy heart by breathing one more requiem above her daughter's resting place. Instinctively Gottlieb withdrew for a little, but when at length her prayer was finished, and she was taking her leave, the fellowship of an overwhelming common sorrow overcame his reserve and emboldened him to lift his hat and say,—

"*Dominus nobiscum.* Before you is a loving daughter's grave, behind me that of a loving sister. Can you tell me how to hold fast my faith in a perfect life in the midst of this darkness of death?"

The startled woman hesitated for a moment, uncertain as to the motive or perhaps the sanity of her questioner. Noticing, however, his gentle sincerity of manner, she kindly answered,—

"Come with me, and I will bring you to a teacher wiser than I."

Silently he followed. Silently they passed the churchyard gate, a few narrow streets, and soon came to the entrance of the Hospital of St. Rupert. The " Brotherhood of the Divine Compassion," under whose charge the hospital was conducted, were at vesper service at the chapel. Pointing to a seat in the rear, the woman hastily withdrew, saying softly, "After service ask for Father Sebastian, and may God send light into thy darkness."

As it happened, it was the first time that Gottlieb had ever been inside a hospital. The world in which he had spent his years was one of sunshine, verdure, growth, forms of beauty, blos-

somings of happy and abounding life. Here
was another world, entirely new—a world of
just the opposite character. Here dwelt human
beings in a light forever shaded, in an air forever
fevered by the hot breath of the diseased.
Here, surrounded by endless varieties of pain
and deformity, each suffering tenant was at this
very moment passing his weary watches amid
sighs and groans or possibly was yielding the
frightful struggle and lapsing into finished
death. At first the horrible thought seemed
more than Gottlieb could well bear. In earlier
days he would certainly have fled the place in
uncontrollable repulsion. Now, however, it
had at least this fascination : it gave a further
vision of the mystery with which his soul was
burdened. Accordingly as the dim altar-lights
struggled with the dim daylight streaming
through the storied windows, and as the chas-
tened voices of the brothers, mingling with the
organ notes, low and accordant, rolled gently
through the chapel arches and melted sooth-
ingly away through the nearer wards to the

ears of the sufferers, Gottlieb was fitted as he
had never before been fitted for a new conception of this mystery of human life and death.

The details of his interview with Father
Sebastian it is needless to rehearse. Of the man,
however, this should be said: namely, that he
was the founder and present spiritual head of
the hospital—a man tall and spare, serious of
face, but withal expressing a kind of sweet con-
tentment not of earth. He, too, in youth had
known the generous aspirations, the passionate
yearnings, of a soul capable of loftiest personal
ideals. And if now to his deep eyes the law of
highest living had come to lie in a domain so
totally antipodal, there were reasons for it in
Father Sebastian's history—reasons deep as the
heart of man, but of which he never spoke. So,
as he kindly conducted Gottlieb to his own cell-
like apartment and turned upon him those dark
eyes that had been opened to the inward blessedness of living not for self-perfecting but for
humblest ministry to others, he took in the history and the needs of the young stranger even

before his story was half told. Still with gentle
sympathy and growing affection, he drew from
the youth all that was upon his heart to utter ;
then gently taking his hand in his own, he
said,—

"Our Lord be praised, my brother, for bringing you to this place of peace, this hospital of
souls as well as of bodies. In this lowly temple
of God's Spirit there is abundant light for all
darkness. Yours is the old but ever-recurring
question, How shall a man actualize the god-
like possibilities of his being—physical, intellec-
tual, spiritual—in a world where blight and
death are perpetually impairing our wisest en-
deavors and thwarting our holiest plans? It
seems, in truth, a staggering question but it so
seems simply because it rests upon false and
partial assumptions. It betrays a fundamental
misconception of perfection itself. Your ideals,
the ideals you have been following these eager
years, are truly beautiful, but they are purely
heathen. Not one of them is loftier than those
of Plato. He taught your principle of living

almost three thousand years ago. Have you
never heard the **voice of** that diviner Teacher
who tells us, 'Whosoever will be great among
you, let him be your minister, and whosoever
will be chief among you, let him be your ser-
vant'? Hitherto you **have lived upon a principle** which, though beautiful and **just in**
appearance, is completely centered in **self.**
Henceforth live upon a new plane, not **for**
personal wisdom or self-enrichment of any sort ;
live only for the good of others. Take Him for
your pattern who **came not to be** ministered
unto but to minister. Only by thus losing your
life can you ever truly find it.''

The appeal had moved the father's heart as
deeply as **it** had **the heart of** Gottlieb. There
was a moment's **silence and** tears stood **in
the** eyes of each as Father Sebastian added, ''**Are
you** equal **to** this, my son ?''

'' **I** will answer you to-morrow,'' said Gottlieb
with a breaking voice **; and,** leaving **upon** the
father's hand a reverent kiss, he hurriedly with-
drew.

Two years from that night Gottlieb is once more in Bingen. He is at home on a visit of unusual interest and he cannot refrain from taking once more an evening walk to the height where stands the church of St. Roch, and from seeking out once more the spot in the homeward way, where in sacred earnestness of soul he had pledged himself to his vanished sister to be a seeker of the highest perfection.

What had happened during these two years? In brief, Father Sebastian's affectionate appeal had been effectual. Between him and the young man so strangely brought to him there had soon sprung up a fellowship of sacred intimacy and depth. The peace and blessedness of soul which Gottlieb saw created and sustained within the hospital by lives of humble ministry, had been to him irrefutable evidence that here was in truth to be found the secret of the perfect life. With characteristic whole-heartedness he had come to the feet of the Divine Teacher, and said, "Teach me the blessedness of living unto others. Let me, like Thyself, be the servant of all." He had begged to be received into the "Brotherhood of the Divine Compassion," and, to the joy of all, had been admitted to the grade of the probationer.

Month by month, under Father Sebastian's enthusiastic guidance, he had studied the lives of the saints—particularly the lives of the more heroic of them, the men who, in order that they might the better serve and save the lives of others, had not counted their lives dear unto themselves. In his new vision, even suffering and disease had come to have a mysterious value, almost a beauty, so potent were they in calling out the most godlike activities of men's souls. Philosophy, æsthetics, poetry, abstract ideas of life—all these things which before had been so dominant within him had fallen into oblivion. At times they recurred to his mind, but he had come to think of them as dreams and to say, "Here is life as it is. Here is action more rational than any of which art or dreamy speculation can tell. Here is knowledge far more human than all they call 'the fair humanities.'"

He had come to see in each new patient a new friend ; and in the gratitude of those he served he found a delight more precious than any his soul had ever tasted.

Thus had swiftly passed the years of his novitiate and now he was here once more beneath the skies of Bingen amid the charmed scenes of his childhood. The sweet melancholy which he had expected to experience from the visit was in his heart. But that was not all. He was troubled, almost alarmed, at the thoughts and feelings which came surging in upon him. In his journey he had passed familiar Heidelberg and, though he had not stopped, it seemed as if a thousand recollections were storming his soul. He had spent a night at Frankfort and as in passing through Hirschgraben Strasse he read upon a door the words, "In this house was born Wolfgang von Goethe," the thought of his sister and of her descriptions of her earlier pilgrimage to this spot had almost unmanned him. At the old home he had found his parents in precarious health, and it had seemed to him as if his father had immediate need of his society and of his aid in business.

Altogether he was in a bewilderment of conflicting emotions ; but that which agitated and alarmed him most of all was the persistent recurrence of thoughts which seemed to bring into his soul unsettlement and doubt with reference to the sacred principle to which he supposed he had unreservedly and irrevocably committed his inmost life. If after his experience he could not believe and rest in the just supremacy of the law of sacrifice and in the beauty of disinterested ministry to the needy, what was there left sacred or true? He feared these diabolic thoughts. Especially did he fear lest they might be proof of some interior rebellion against the lifelong vows he was about to assume. Had his moral enthusiasm, his spirit of holy consecration, deserted him? Was he flagging in the good way? He chided himself; he wept; he sought to pray but the heavens seemed brazen. At last, with an almost guilty feeling, he desperately exclaimed,

"I cannot drive these troubling thoughts away. I must have it out with them. Why should I fear?"

So he seated himself by the wayside, hard by the spot where to his exultant sister he had sworn his first great vow and there he bade his strange new thoughts speak out their worst. And his thoughts said, "Why have you given yourself up to this unreason? Why are you standing on the threshold of a life which can be but a living death? Say not it is the voice of right. What right has any human creature to cast away the precious opportunities which God is trying to give him? Put yourself in God's place. You are trying to carry the possibilities of a higher intelligence and larger life to those two orphan lads whom you last week began to teach to read. Would you be pleased to have them reject all further opportunities and reject your instruction on the ground, forsooth, that they ought not to be working for their own benefit but only for the good of others? You have no right to take your life into your own hands and dedicate it to the archangel Michael or to any of his angels. What better right have you to take it into your hands and devote it to the service of this man John or that woman Margaret or to any rabble of Johns and Margarets? Moreover, your rule itself is self-destructive. If every man were to live simply to serve others, there would be nobody left to be served, and so the very triumph of your rule would be its destruction. If you say you would have every man live to serve others, yet in such a spirit as to be willing to receive like service from others, you thereby totally shift your ground. You abandon your senseless rule of living solely to serve, and adopt the reasonable principle of mutual reciprocity. Why, then, longer sophisticate yourself? Why sacrifice to natures of small possibility natures of the greatest? In God's clear sight your good is just as precious as the good of any human being. Hence what He commands and desires is not that you love your neighbor better than yourself but that you love your neighbor as yourself. Will you be wiser than God?"

By this time Gottlieb trembled in every limb ;
but he would not surrender. "Back, ye lying
thoughts!" he cried. "Away! I cannot, I
will not listen. You fain would shake me by
your reasonings, but I know your reasonings
well. They are as old as the evil world. They
are as plausible ás the reciprocity of publicans
and sinners, who lend one to another, hoping to
receive the same again. I have been schooled
by a diviner Teacher, one who bids me give,
hoping for nothing again. I am a learner at
the feet of Him who said, 'If any man will be
great among you, let him be your minister.'"

Thereat the evil thoughts again arose and
made new onset. They cried, "Out of your
own mouth will we confute you. Nay, out of
the very mouth of your Teacher and Lord.
What says He? 'If any man *would be great*
among you let him be your servant.' What
could be plainer? Serving is not life's end, it is
simply a means. The man who would be great
is not rebuked, he is encouraged. He is told the

means by which he may achieve this greatness.
If you see **in** this 'Brotherhood of the Divine
Compassion' the best field for developing your
powers and becoming to the best of your
possibilities **great and commanding,** all is well.
It is not against service as a means **to personal**
improvement and perfection **that we protest,**
only against service as an end, a service which
makes servile. Let personal growth, culture,
advancement, realization of your supreme possibilities be made your aim and hospital service
the means, and you will have harmonized
your first life theory with your second.
You will have removed the conflict. You can
then be just to Plato without disloyalty to
Christ.''

This time **Gottlieb** was silent. **He** could not
reply. He felt his mind was still **in** darkness.
But it was as if some great **truth were** dawning
over him, the light of which would compel a
revision of his plan of life. He waited and
waited for the dawning, **but it still delayed to**
come. **At** last, as the Bingen church bells

struck the hour of midnight, he rose and started for his home.

Calmed yet unrested by the contest with his boisterous thoughts, he said to himself, "Four rules of life I see, four principles of personal living. I began with the first. I said I would live to grow, to develop, to seek my highest possible perfection. The essential selfishness of this was later shown to me. I was taught the precious secret of the second principle, that of living not to be ministered unto but to minister. Now I see this third, which says, 'Live to become perfect, but serve your fellow men so far as this serving can help to make you great and perfect.' Beyond all these I see a fourth, a principle which just reverses the third and says, 'Grow, seek all possible personal improvement in order that in the end you may the better serve your needy fellows.' Here ministry is the end, the pursuit of personal perfection the means thereto. Which of the four is right? Sister Gretchen, Father Sebastian, I am still a child! Who now shall lead me? Who now shall light my darkness?"

A week later he had written a letter that
caused profound grief to Father Sebastian and
had suddenly started for the Holy Land.

The thought of visiting the scenes of sacred
history had come to Gottlieb's mind like an
inspiration. The struggle of soul through which
he had just come was the severest of his life.
The suggestions and perplexities with which he
had wrestled seemed to him in part so sinister
and diabolic that though he had struggled
through to a clear and unwavering conviction
that, with his views, duty called him to break
with the Brotherhood, he was yet left with a
sense of defeat and humiliation. Moreover, to
break with the man to whom he owed so great
a spiritual debt, a man so unselfishly noble as
Father Sebastian, his only inmost friend, had
left his heart sore and bleeding. He felt it
would be good to go and press the footprints of
the Man of Sorrows, and to remember the
greater griefs He bore. The idea first occurred

to his mind that terrible night at Bingen. As
he entered his old home, he thought of his
sister's pilgrimage. He said, " If she could take
such pains to get herself in closer acquaintance-
ship with Goethe, why should not I follow my
diviner Teacher from His birthplace to His
grave? Where else shall I be as likely to find
light and comfort for my baffled spirit, solution
for my yet unanswered problem?"

It was a happy thought. Already, before he
saw the sacred mountains, while yet his steamer
panted across the blue Levant eastward, his
spirits rose within him. The dark struggles at
Bingen seemed more and more a frightful night-
mare, out of which he had now waked into a
world as full of sparkling beauty as was that in
which he had reveled ere yet Gretchen's death
had suddenly darkened all things. A sacred
elation of spirit took possession of him, and as
he came to holy Bethlehem he was as one who
dreams. The Gospels now became his hourly
study. The youth of the world was lived over
in the old patriarchal resting places. The Bible,

illuminated by storied landscapes and **Abra-
hamic** stars, became a new and vivid revelation.
The mountain-climbing, the long equestrian
and pedestrian **marches, the changed fare,** the
new knowledge, the keen emotions, healed the
thought-sick **brain and soothed the wounded
heart.** Only **rarely,** when his thoughts turned
from the happy present to scan the unknown
future, was there **for** a moment some inward
shadow of fear. What unexpected deliverance
from this shadow awaited him can best be told
by himself in an extract from **a letter** written to
Father Sebastian some years afterwards. The
extract is as **follows :**

"To-day, my **precious friend, I** have received
official **notification of my appointment to** the
chair of Christian ethics in my old University
of Heidelberg. At once **I** think of you and
take my pen to commune with you, not because
I wish your kindly congratulations, but because
I have never told you of the great solution I
found in **the Holy** Land for all that wretched
problem of normal living, **in view** of which I

was constrained to disappoint you and the dear brothers who toil with you in your divinely beautiful ministry to human pain and woe. The solution was given me in a manner so unexpected and providential that I must give you the full details.

"One day, toward the end of my pilgrimage, I was traveling—on horseback of course—in the mountains of Lebanon on the trail from Damascus to Beyroot. Here I encountered one of those events which worldlings call accidents. Over a deep-down mountain stream was one of the rude bridges of the region, constructed of two logs laid from bank to bank, with flat stones on them and a little earth above to constitute a path. My two companions, who were commercial travelers from Smyrna, rode over in safety; but as I was bringing up the rear, one of the stones was so struck by my horse's hoof, that it turned suddenly over, precipitating horse and rider into the rocky stream-bed ten feet below. One of my legs was broken, and the horse so injured that it became necessary to shoot him where he fell.

"Happily I had learned at Damascus of an American mission station at Zahleh, upon this very route, and to this my companions succeeded in transporting me before resuming their journey. The village we found had a pleasant situation, well up the eastern slope of a long range of foothills, but like all North Syrian villages it seemed built for cattle rather than for human beings. The earth-floored houses had stone and mud for walls, wood and stone and mud for roofs. In one of the best the missionary and his family gave me most Christian welcome. I was quickly placed upon a comfortable bed and whatever was best in the house was placed at my disposal. Of course my old experience with you in caring for the wounded now served me in an unexpected manner. I was able to give all necessary directions relative to the setting and dressing of my shattered limb and in a short time was made almost as comfortable as if I had been in the dear old hospital of St. Rupert. Days and nights of torture, however, followed;

and after this the weariness of a slow convalescence. For a time I wondered if such a novice in the school of suffering as I was could ever endure the pains, but in the end I found that our Lord had prepared me a table in the wilderness.

"During my convalescence I had abundant time to study my new surroundings. The missionary I found was a native of New England, a tall, wiry man, of evident strength of character and purpose. His wife, though of gentler mold, was of remarkable intelligence in all that relates to the Bible, to personal religion, and to the present religious condition of the world. Every morning and every evening, with their children, they had family worship—a custom of which I had heard, but which I now for the first time witnessed. One thing specially struck me, namely, that every Sunday evening, as if to lighten the labors of the husband, the family devotions were conducted by the wife. On other days the missionary, in visiting his schools and families, was compelled to be absent most of the time so that with the three children I was left largely to the companionship and care of the pious mother. Often she would have the oldest child read to me from some English work found in their scanty library. At other times she would discuss with me beautiful English hymns, many of which she knew by heart. One afternoon, when I was so far improved as to be sitting outside the door, where I was gazing my fill at the distant sunlit Anti-Lebanon, she brought a thick book from the long shelf above the table and asked me if ever I had heard of Jonathan Edwards of New England and his saintly wife. I had to confess that I had not. She then told me that by many European theologians he was considered the most subtle and powerful theological thinker the New World had yet produced. She added that he was born the same year as John Wesley, and that while the one called the perfect life 'Christian virtue' and the other called it 'Christian perfection,' the two wonderfully agreed as to its blessedness.

"'Perfection?' said I, withdrawing my gaze from the mountains. 'I began my life a seeker after perfection but, alas! too soon I discovered that I knew not the way. What mean *you* by Christian perfection?'

"'Let me read you the experience of Edwards and the definition of Wesley,' she replied.

"'No,' said I, impatiently, 'I want none of your professional experiences and professional definitions. I cannot help thinking how your theologians are all the time considering what they will write, and what people will think of the writer. No, I want a living utterance of a living soul. You have come out here, half across the world, to teach blind men the secret of the perfect life. I know it from your prayers. I am one who seeks, and long have sought, precisely this knowledge. I am in greater need of it than any of these half-barbarians for whom you and your husband are laboring. They are simply uninstructed: I am bewildered, baffled, despairing. Tell me in one word *your* theory, *your* law of a perfect human living.'

"My sudden impetuosity as I closed frightened me, for I feared it would frighten her. Her eyes did certainly grow great with a kind of awe as she lifted them for a moment to study my expression, but she showed no sign of hesitation.

"'Theodore,' she said, turning to the little boy at her feet, 'what is the first and great commandment?'

"Theodore looked up from the playthings before him and answered, '"Thou shalt love the Lord thy God with all thy heart, and with all thy soul, and with all thy mind, and with all thy strength." You taught me that last Sunday.'

"'And what else did I teach you, dear?'

"'He that feareth is not made perfect in love.'

"Kissing the boy for his faithful memorizing, she silently rose from her chair, re-entered the house, and commenced preparations for the evening meal.

"For a time I was piqued and amazed that to

so personal and passionate an appeal this Christian woman had made so impersonal and evasive a response. By and by, however, when the evening was over and the silent hours of slumber were in the house, I reviewed the whole scene and slowly recalled each word that each of us had spoken. Then, as I pondered the final words by the lips of the child, a strange and awful light began to creep over my spirit. I said to myself, 'Why have I never asked myself what is God's first, last, and ever-present demand upon this life of mine? What form of perfection has He who made me set before me? To what would He have me aspire? What if it should turn out that, being made for God, a man can have no perfection but in God? What if this perfect love which casteth out all fear should be the secret of the perfect life? If so, what wonder if the man who loves not utterly, absolutely, perfectly, unremittingly, misses the principle of all true living?'

"Awed by these new thoughts, my heart stood still. Too well I knew I did not love,

had never loved, **my** Maker with that **passion
which** would make His absence death, His
presence life. Too well I saw that all my plans
of life, my **motives** of action, had been but self-
evolved, self-centered, **and** self-respecting. I
had sought no sanction for them **higher than**
my own subjective approval. What I **had done,**
I had done unto myself, and not **unto Him** in
whom and for whom I should have held my
being. The revelation appalled **me** beyond
anything I had ever encountered. I poured out
hot tears of contrition. I called upon God for
mercy and for that perfect love which should
cast out every fear.

"How long this storm of spirit lasted, **I never
knew; but at last there came** to my agitated
bosom an assurance **of** divine compassion that
made me feel as if celestial doors had opened,
and as if through **them I had passed** into the
very vestibule of the heavenly state. **Whether
it was a vision** or a heaven-sent dream, **I know
not; but some way it** seemed as if suddenly I
were walking a transfigured Rhineland, and as

if beside me I beheld transfigured Gretchen
with eyes full of a larger wisdom than I had
seen there in my boyhood. And ere she spoke
one word of the loving greetings with which
every feature was radiant, she exclaimed, 'Love,
my Gottlieb, love is the secret of perfect living.
Before my Goethe pilgrimage was ended, I discovered thirsts of spirit which Goethe could not
satisfy. I died too suddenly to let you know
the better shrines I sought and found. But of
your noble questionings, strivings, struggles, I
have not been kept in ignorance. To your early
quest of personal perfection, one thing alone
was lacking—it lacked the elevation, the consecration, the emancipation which a perfect
love of God, all perfect, would have given you.
Your second endeavor, your self-dedication to a
humble and self-denying ministry to your
fellow men, what lacked it but the saving
motive of love, that Godward love which would
have made it a holier ministry, a self-offering
unto Christ your Lord?

"'Your other baffling questions as to ends

and means—as to whether **men should make the most of themselves in** order then the better **to serve or, on the contrary,** first serve their **fellow men in order in the end to gain** thereby **the greater self-enrichment and** to come the nearer to perfection—what were **these but questionings of purblind** self-consideration—problems which could never once have thrust themselves upon any self-abandoning, self-forgetting **lover of his God? In love, love** of the **All**-perfect, **love of the one** Lover, every noble **principle of human living** is taken up, every **ideal** transfigured, supplemented, glorified. **Henceforth thou** knowest the perfect way.'

"**At last morning dawned and a new day,** the brightest **I** had **ever seen. By** previous appointment friends from Beyroot **came** to take me to the Thursday steamer. It **was hard to** say farewell to such **a** Bethel-home. **How newly,** freshly fair appeared to me at morning **prayers** that **pair of lovers of my Lord, in** exile from their **kindred, in order** that, **for** love of God and man, they might teach benighted souls the secret of a life divinely beautiful. In taking my leave I could not restrain tears of gratitude ; and though I could not tell them of my vision, I could and did assure them that through their influence a life hopeless and bewildered had found rest and healing. And when I had given a farewell kiss to little Theodore, I saw a strange up-lighting of his mother's eyes, as I solemnly added, 'Out of the mouth of babes and sucklings, hast thou ordained strength.'

"My dear Sebastian, here my letter must be ended. The problem I first brought you, together with all the dark, entangling questions which went before and after,—all are answered. The solution of all details of duty and of aspiration is as simple as in nature the law of gravitation. I gravitate forever toward my God. Better than that, I am already in my God and He in me. We possess a mutual life, a life in which all petty self-directions and self-seekings cease. By His own spirit I am guided ever more fully, ever more blessedly, into all truth.

"Pathfinding in this mazy world is indeed a

serious matter to him who looks at paths **alone.**
But high above all **paths is** He who makes them
all, and any soul that has the **one** Pathmaker
as his ever-present leader leaves pathfinding to
the blind and lost. **Pray for me that in the**
academic halls to which my **Lord has just now**
brought **me, I may show** this light **to** thou-
sands. Pray that at the base of lovely Koenigsstuhl I may teach my youthful countrymen the
precious mystery taught me at the base of holy
Lebanon."

Here ends the **letter to** Father Sebastian, **and**
here also ends the story of our Gottlieb.

www.ingramcontent.com/pod-product-compliance
Lightning Source LLC
Chambersburg PA
CBHW022202020726
47496CB00008B/2841